DISCOVER SERIES
LOS CACHORROS

Pastor Australiano

Basset Hound

Beagle

Bulldog

Chihuahua

Chow Chow

Cocker Spaniel

Dachshund o Perro salchicha

Doberman Pinscher

Pastor Alemán

Gran Danes

Pit Bull terrier americano

Pomerania

Caniche

Doguillo

Rottweiler

Terrier escoces

Shih Tzu

Springer Spaniel Ingles

Caniche enano

Braco de Weimar

Labrador Amarillo

Yorkshire Terrier

Make Sure to Check Out the Other Discover Series Books from Xist Publishing:

Published in the United States by Xist Publishing
www.xistpublishing.com
PO Box 61593 Irvine, CA 92602

© 2018 by Xist Publishing All rights reserved
Translated by Lenny Sandoval
No portion of this book may be reproduced without express permission of the publisher
All images licensed from Fotolia
First Spanish Edition

ISBN: 978-1-5324-0776-5   eISBN: 978-1-5324-0777-2

xist Publishing

www.ingramcontent.com/pod-product-compliance
Lightning Source LLC
LaVergne TN
LVHW070950070426
835507LV00030B/3485